Magical Magnificat

Written and illustrated by

Sarah and Evelyn Vaughan

This book belongs to

_____

Draw a picture of yourself
here.

In loving memory of Thelma and Peter Wrathall and their mischievous, magical cat.

Magical Magnificat woke up
one sunny day,
She stretched and yawned
and stretched again,
And went outside to play.

She went to see some children who were playing in the park.
Swinging, sliding, running, climbing, having such a lark.
She took some time to run around and make friends with a bee,
Then looked around and up and down to see what she could see.

What do you think can she see? What can you see where you are right now?

Magnificat purred
goodbye and wandered
into town,
She liked to meet the
people there and listen
to the sounds.
Ears up, head high, she
listened in to see what
she could hear,
Music, talking, people
walking and traffic far
and near.

What else do you think
she can hear? What
can you hear?

She wandered through the market stalls, so colourful and bright.
She sniffed the air and took deep breaths, the smells were a delight:
Coffee from the coffee stand and fresh bread from the bakers,
Flowers from the flower stall and spicy curry makers.

What's your favourite smell?

She visited the fishmonger,
who knew her very well.
She sat outside and licked
her lips at the fishy-liscious
smell!
He saw his friend and gave
a smile and went to find a
dish,
Then came to give
Magnificat a very tasty fish.

What's your favourite food?
What does it taste like?

Magnificat was full up now and feeling rather tired,
A snuggle in her favourite spot was certainly required.
She went home to her owner, who softly stroked her back.
They settled in an armchair for their afternoon cat nap.

Where is your favourite place to snuggle up? Do you have a cosy blanket or a soft pillow that you like to lie on?

Magnificat

Magical Magnificat dreamed
a marvellous dream,
Of all the things she'd done
today and the people she
had seen.
The sights and smells, the
tasty fish, the lap where she
now lay.
Magical Magnificat had had
a magic day.

What did you do today that
made you feel magical?

A young Sarah and Magnificat.

The original Magnificat belonged to Sarah's Grandparents when she was a child, and was a much loved, mischievous cat. She was always doing funny things from the day she arrived as a small grey fluffy kitten. Her antics included climbing the Christmas tree, regularly, knocking it to the floor and then chasing the baubles; jumping on the piano keys making a terrible sound and scaring the life out of the poor cleaner, who thought she was in the house alone; and jumping up on the chair besides Sarah's grandmother when a mouse ran across the kitchen floor!

She was not your average cat and that is why she was such an inspiration for this story.

Can you draw some friends
for Magical Magnificat?

Draw a picture of a place that you think Magical Magnificat might like to visit.

What might she see, hear, smell and taste?

Wordsearch

M	H	B	U	R	T	C	A	O	D	I
P	A	M	F	S	O	A	E	K	X	M
R	P	G	E	Q	Y	L	T	B	F	A
E	P	U	N	L	S	M	A	R	E	G
L	Y	T	R	I	L	P	E	A	Z	I
A	O	D	U	E	F	F	G	L	E	N
X	A	Z	W	M	Y	I	N	W	L	A
E	K	J	M	A	G	I	C	S	H	T
D	F	R	I	E	N	D	S	A	U	I
P	S	A	O	B	Q	E	B	V	T	O
M	I	N	D	F	U	L	W	Y	C	N

Can you find these words hidden in this wordsearch?

MAGNIFICAT   CALM

RELAXED   FRIENDS

MAGIC   MINDFUL

IMAGINATION   HAPPY

Can you make your own wordsearch?

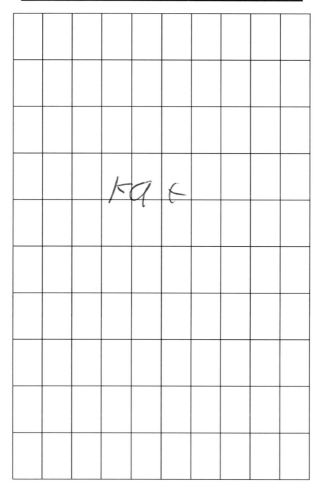

Write the words to search for below.

Printed in Great Britain
by Amazon

72726500R00015